THE
HOLY
TWINS

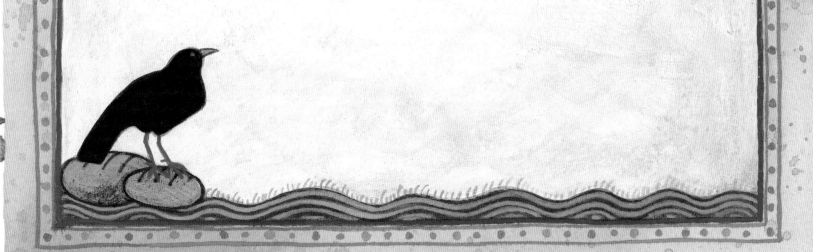

THE
HOLY
TWINS

BENEDICT AND SCHOLASTICA

WRITTEN BY

Kathleen Norris

ILLUSTRATED BY

Tomie dePaola

G. P. PUTNAM'S SONS

The author would like to thank
her Benedictine friends
for their hospitality and prayers.

—K. N.

For the Benedictine communities of
the Abbey of Regina Laudis
and Weston Priory,
especially Rt. Rev. Mother Benedict,
Mother Placid, Mother Dolores,
Brother John and Brother Elias.

Also for Jack Shanhaar
and in memory of Lauren Ford
and Father Bede Scholz,
who all taught me the Benedictine way:
that my work is my prayer.

And, of course, for Mario.

—T. deP.

The letters *C. S. P. B.*
on the Cross of St. Benedict stand for
Crux Sancti Patris Benedicti.
"Cross of the Holy Father Benedict."

MANY hundreds of years ago, in the small town of Nursia, in the mountains of northern Italy, there lived a twin brother and a sister named Benedict and Scholastica.

ENJOYING the run of their family land, Benedict and Scholastica climbed trees, fed stray cats and raced each other to the tops of hills.

Day in, day out, they were inseparable, and anyone would have said they were the best of friends. But they also squabbled loudly, especially when Benedict would make up too many rules for their games and Scholastica would laugh and ignore them.

THEIR family was an ancient and well-respected one, and the custom of that time was for young noblemen such as Benedict to be sent to study in the great city of Rome, while girls received an education closer to home.

So when the time came for Benedict to go to Rome, Scholastica was sent to live in a monastery of nuns in Nursia, where she learned to read and write.

BENEDICT and Scholastica were sad to be separated, but Scholastica was comforted by the women of her new community and was eager to help them fulfill Jesus' command to feed and clothe the poor and to tend the sick. She also loved the prayers that the women sang every day. She missed Benedict very much and prayed that even though she could no longer look on her brother's face, she would never leave his heart.

BENEDICT loved learning
all that a young nobleman was
expected to learn: Greek, Latin,
writing, law. But he missed his sister
Scholastica and the hills of Umbria.
He longed to tell Scholastica all that
he saw in the great city, which was
noisy and crowded compared with
home. Benedict was troubled by the
cruelty he witnessed there, and the
way that slaves were treated as
property rather than human beings.

BENEDICT realized that while Rome held great opportunities for his success, there were also many dangers to his soul. Competition among his fellow students had grown so fierce that they no longer trusted one another. Even Christian clergy were tempted by power, and rival factions would battle over possession of the churches. Benedict found this deeply disturbing and was grateful for the prayers of his sister.

Although his family expected him to finish his studies and become a well-paid civil official, Benedict began to desire a quieter, simpler life. He left the city for a rural village, where he joined a small group that spent each day reading the Scriptures, praying the Psalms and doing honest labor to support themselves.

S O O N, however, Benedict began to feel that God was calling him to live all alone so that he could devote nearly all his time to prayer. He struck out on his own, and as he neared the lake of Subiaco, seeking a place that was wild and remote, he met a monk named Romanus, who gave him a monk's robe and told him of a cave nearby.

Once Benedict was settled there, Romanus began to sneak out of his own monastery, against the rules, to take food to the young hermit. Benedict's cave was at the base of a steep cliff, and Romanus had to lower the food in a bundle tied to a sturdy rope. He attached a little bell to the rope so that Benedict would know that a gift of food was coming.

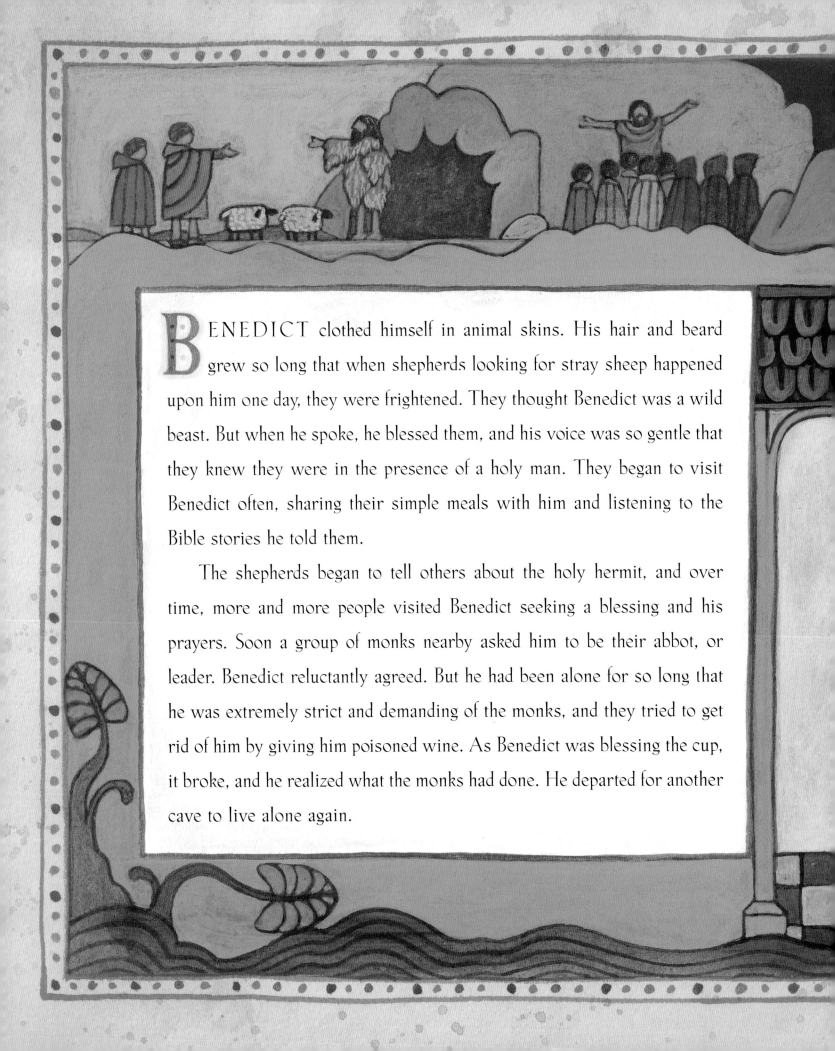

BENEDICT clothed himself in animal skins. His hair and beard grew so long that when shepherds looking for stray sheep happened upon him one day, they were frightened. They thought Benedict was a wild beast. But when he spoke, he blessed them, and his voice was so gentle that they knew they were in the presence of a holy man. They began to visit Benedict often, sharing their simple meals with him and listening to the Bible stories he told them.

The shepherds began to tell others about the holy hermit, and over time, more and more people visited Benedict seeking a blessing and his prayers. Soon a group of monks nearby asked him to be their abbot, or leader. Benedict reluctantly agreed. But he had been alone for so long that he was extremely strict and demanding of the monks, and they tried to get rid of him by giving him poisoned wine. As Benedict was blessing the cup, it broke, and he realized what the monks had done. He departed for another cave to live alone again.

BUT Benedict's reputation as a holy man spread far and wide, and soon twelve small monasteries had sprung up around him. Three were high on a mountain, and the monks had to climb up and down its steep slopes every day to get water from the lake.

One day they asked Benedict if they could move nearer the lake. Benedict said nothing, but went with a young monk named Placid to the top of the mountain, where he prayed for hours. As he left, he put three stones on the spot. The next day he told the monks that at the place where they would find three stones, God had provided a spring of water. And indeed, that stream flows down the mountainside to this day.

THE city of Rome had become even more violent since Benedict had left it, and noble families of the city began sending their sons to Benedict to receive instruction in the Bible and in prayer. Young Placid was one such student and Maurus was another.

One hot, lazy afternoon when Placid was sent to fetch water, he carelessly dropped his bucket into the lake and fell in after it. A strong current soon swept him far from shore. Benedict, who was praying in his room, knew in his heart what had happened, and he quickly summoned Maurus and told him to go to Placid's rescue. Maurus asked Benedict to bless him and then he ran out of the monastery as fast as he could.

PAX

MAURUS was so intent on saving Placid that he didn't stop running when he came to the shore, but raced across the water and pulled poor Placid up by his hair! Not until the two young men were safely back on land did Maurus realize what he had done.

"I didn't do it. I couldn't have," he said, amazed. "It must have been the abbot's doing!"

Benedict told Maurus that it was his readiness to obey that had caused the miracle. Then Placid spoke up and said that as Maurus was pulling him out of the water, he had not seen Maurus, but rather the hood of the abbot's habit above him.

TALES such as this one spread throughout the region, making a local priest jealous. Pretending to be a friend, he gave Benedict some poisoned bread. As Benedict was about to taste it, a raven swooped down and knocked the bread from Benedict's hand. He took this as a sign that he should move on.

BENEDICT went to the top of a high mountain, Monte Cassino, where he founded a monastery for men who wished to live in harmony with one another and with their God. The disorder and injustice that had troubled Benedict in Rome had made the city vulnerable to invasion, and for many years the monks watched armies advancing and retreating in the valley. Their monastery became a place of refuge for peasants and nobles alike.

AFTER Benedict had settled at Monte Cassino, he and his sister Scholastica decided to meet once a year. She traveled with a group of nuns to the gatehouse of the monastery, and Benedict would come down the mountain with several monks.

As Benedict told his sister about everything that had happened to him since he left for Rome, Scholastica decided that she liked the gentle man her brash young twin had become. He had learned much, she decided, from his many trials. He was no longer impatient with those who were not as smart or quick as himself. And Benedict admitted that his experiences had taught him to be more kind than strict.

Then Benedict told Scholastica that he was writing a rule that he hoped would help his monks to pray, work and live together in peace. He said he wanted a commonsense rule that real people could live with, one that would give them room to experiment and even to fail, and then, with the help of God, learn from their mistakes, as he hoped he had done.

SCHOLASTICA was impressed but also secretly amused. Or not so secretly, and she began to giggle. So much of what he had told her, she said, sounded like things she had learned by trial and error in her own monastery. And, she added, really laughing now, "Isn't it funny, Brother, that you had to travel all over Italy to learn some of the things that I discovered by staying in one place!"

Then she offered wise advice. "Brother," she said, "as the leader of the monastery, one must listen to others with the 'ear of the heart.'"

ROTHER and sister looked forward to their yearly meetings. Usually Scholastica and her sisters would depart in the afternoon, but one day Benedict and Scholastica became so wrapped up in their talking that they did not notice that the sun was setting. Benedict did not want to spend the night away from his monastery, but Scholastica desired to continue the holy conversation with her brother. Exasperated, her brother replied, "Sister, what are you saying? It is completely impossible for me to remain outside my monastery."

AT the time he said this, there was not a cloud in the evening sky. But when her brother refused her, Scholastica began to pray with her fingers intertwined and her head resting on her hands. When she raised her head, violent thunder and lightning erupted outside. Scholastica's face was wet with tears and rain poured from the heavens. The more she wept, the more it rained. Benedict realized that he would not be able to climb the mountain to his monastery that night.

Not for the first time in his life, he cried out, "Sister, what have you done? May God forgive you!"

And, as sassy as the girl who had scrapped with him in childhood, Scholastica replied, "You wouldn't listen to me, but God did. Go now, if you can, back to your monastery!"

Benedict, knowing he was beaten, stayed with his sister, praying and talking all night.

T H E monks were surprised to see Benedict give in. But the very next day, when they told their brethren about the miraculous rain, the monks began to realize that it had been caused by love. Scholastica's desire to see her brother was stronger than his desire to follow a regulation, because as the Gospel of John puts it, "God is love," and Scholastica was able to do more because she loved more.

Three days after her visit, Benedict saw the soul of Scholastica rising to heaven in the form of a dove. Overcome with emotion and grateful for their last visit together, he shed tears of his own. And after announcing her death to the monks, he sent for her body so that it might be laid in the tomb that he had prepared for himself.

SOON after Scholastica's death Benedict had another vision. He was praying in the middle of the night when he saw the entire world being gathered up into a single ray of light. Dark and light, Earth and heaven, were all one in God's sight, and it was a wondrous sight indeed.

NOT long afterward, Benedict sensed that his death was approaching. He asked his fellow monks to carry him to the church, where he died as the monks prayed over him. At that very moment, monks in another monastery saw a vision of Benedict walking on a road of light that led from his monastery room to heaven.

His body was placed, as he had asked, in the tomb with his beloved sister Scholastica. As Gregory the Great wrote in *Life and Miracles of St. Benedict*, "In this way it happened that those two whose minds were always united in God were not separated in body by the grave."

THE AMAZING RULE OF ST. BENEDICT

THE RULE that Benedict wrote over 1,500 years ago made such good sense that it is still being used today by Christian monks and nuns who live in monasteries in all corners of the world. They are known as Benedictines or Cistercians (also nicknamed "Trappists"), and their tradition of hospitality continues to make visitors feel welcome.

Benedict's rule consists of a prologue and 73 chapters based on the Bible, especially the Psalms and Gospels. Benedict also drew on his own experiences as a monk and the wisdom of earlier monastic rules. From a fourth century Egyptian monk named Pachomius, who had once been centurion (the leader of a hundred men) in the Roman Army, Benedict became convinced of the importance of regular hours for prayers, meals and work. Pachomius had run his monastery like an army, even using trumpeters to awaken the community at the same early hour each morning. Benedict assigned one monk to rouse the others in the morning, a practice that continues in monasteries to this day and continues to make sleepy monks grumble. Some scholars believe that monks may be credited with inventing the alarm clock.

From a Greek monk named Basil, Benedict learned that monks should try to be sober and dignified in all that they do, because God is present everywhere and sees all our actions. Benedict also realized that if the Almighty is truly everywhere, we might find God in unexpected places: in the sick, in the poor, and in children (who were not much respected in the time that Benedict lived). Even visitors who interrupted the monastery's routine, Benedict said, were to be "received as Christ" and treated as if they were a gift from God.

From the rule of a monk known only as "The Master," Benedict learned how not to treat people—as if they would do something wrong the minute his back was turned. The Master, for example, required that monks who had finished their work do "busy work" because if they were idle they would only get into trouble. In contrast, Benedict scheduled time each day for play. These days, Benedictine monks and nuns might use their recreation time to go for hikes, do puzzles, play cards or watch a video together.

Many people who are not monks or nuns have found that Benedict's Rule offers good, practical advice and spiritual counsel for getting along with others in a family, on the job, or in a church community.

CHAPTER 2: WHAT KIND OF MAN THE ABBOT OUGHT TO BE.

CHAPTER 16: HOW THE WORK OF GOD IS TO BE PERFORMED DURING THE DAY.

CHAPTER 53: ON THE RECEPTION OF GUESTS.

PAX

CHAPTER 72: ON THE GOOD ZEAL WHICH MONKS OUGHT TO HAVE.

If you would like to know more about Benedict, Scholastica
and the Rule, these books might be of interest:

Benedict, Saint, Abbot of Monte Cassino. *RB 1980: The Rule of St. Benedict.*
Edited by Timothy Fry. Collegeville, Minn.: Liturgical Press, 1981.

Chittister, Joan. *Wisdom Distilled from the Daily: Living the Rule of St. Benedict Today.*
San Francisco: Harper & Row, 1990.

de Waal, Esther. *Living with Contradiction: Reflections on the Rule of St. Benedict.*
San Francisco: Harper & Row, 1989.

de Waal, Esther. *Seeking God: The Way of St. Benedict.*
Collegeville, Minn.: Liturgical Press, 1984.

Gregory the Great. *Life and Miracles of St. Benedict: Book Two of the Dialogues.*
Translated by Odo J. Zimmermann and Benedict R. Avery.
Westport, Conn.: Greenwood Press, 1980.

Stewart, Columba. *Prayer and Community: The Benedictine Tradition.*
Maryknoll, N.Y.: Orbis Books, 1998.

Text copyright © 2001 by Kathleen Norris
Illustrations copyright © 2001 by Tomie dePaola
All rights reserved.
This book, or parts thereof, may not be reproduced in any form without permission in writing from the publisher,
G. P. PUTNAM'S SONS
a division of Penguin Putnam Books for Young Readers, 345 Hudson Street, New York, NY 10014.
G. P. Putnam's Sons, Reg. U.S. Pat. & Tm. Off. Published simultaneously in Canada.
Printed in Hong Kong by South China Printing Co. (1988) Ltd.
Designed by Cecilia Yung and Sharon Jacobs. The text was set in 15-point Phaistos.
The art was done in acrylics on tea-stained 140 lb. Arches cold-pressed watercolor paper.
Library of Congress Cataloging-in-Publication Data
Norris, Kathleen, 1947–
The holy twins : Benedict and Scholastica / written by Kathleen Norris;
illustrated by Tomie dePaola.
p. cm. 1. Benedict, Saint, Abbot of Monte Cassino—Juvenile literature.
2. Scholastica, Saint, 6th cent.—Juvenile literature.
3. Christian saints—Italy—Biography—Juvenile literature.
[1. Benedict, Saint, Abbot of Monte Cassino. 2. Scholastica, Saint, 6th cent. 3. Saints.]
I. De Paola, Tomie, ill. II. Title.
BR1720.B45 N67 2001 271'.102—dc21 [B] 00-040294
ISBN 0-399-23424-1
1 3 5 7 9 10 8 6 4 2
FIRST IMPRESSION